THE DARK KNIGHT

HarperCollins®, ⬥®, and HarperEntertainment™
are trademarks of HarperCollins Publishers.

The Dark Knight: Batman Saves the Day
BATMAN and all related characters
and elements are trademarks of DC Comics © 2008.
All rights reserved. Printed in the United States of America.
No part of this book may be used or reproduced in any manner
whatsoever without written permission except in the case of
brief quotations embodied in critical articles and reviews.
For information address HarperCollins Children's Books,
a division of HarperCollins Publishers,
1350 Avenue of the Americas, New York, NY 10019.
www.harpercollinschildrens.com

Library of Congress catalog card number: 2008922486
ISBN 978-0-06-156187-0

Book design by John Sazaklis
❖
First Edition

THE DARK KNIGHT™

BATMAN
SAVES THE DAY

ADAPTED BY **JENNIFER FRANTZ**

PENCILS BY **CAMERON STEWART**

DIGITAL PAINTS BY **DAVE McCAIG**

INSPIRED BY THE FILM **THE DARK KNIGHT**

SCREENPLAY BY **JONATHAN NOLAN**
AND **CHRISTOPHER NOLAN**

STORY BY **CHRISTOPHER NOLAN** & **DAVID S. GOYER**

BATMAN CREATED BY **BOB KANE**

HarperEntertainment
An Imprint of HarperCollinsPublishers

Rachel Dawes looked around her Gotham City apartment. It was decorated with flowers and streamers. "Perfect!" she said as she placed one last vase of roses on the table. Everything was ready for the big party.

Rachel couldn't wait to surprise her friend Bruce Wayne for his birthday. And the guests would be arriving any minute.

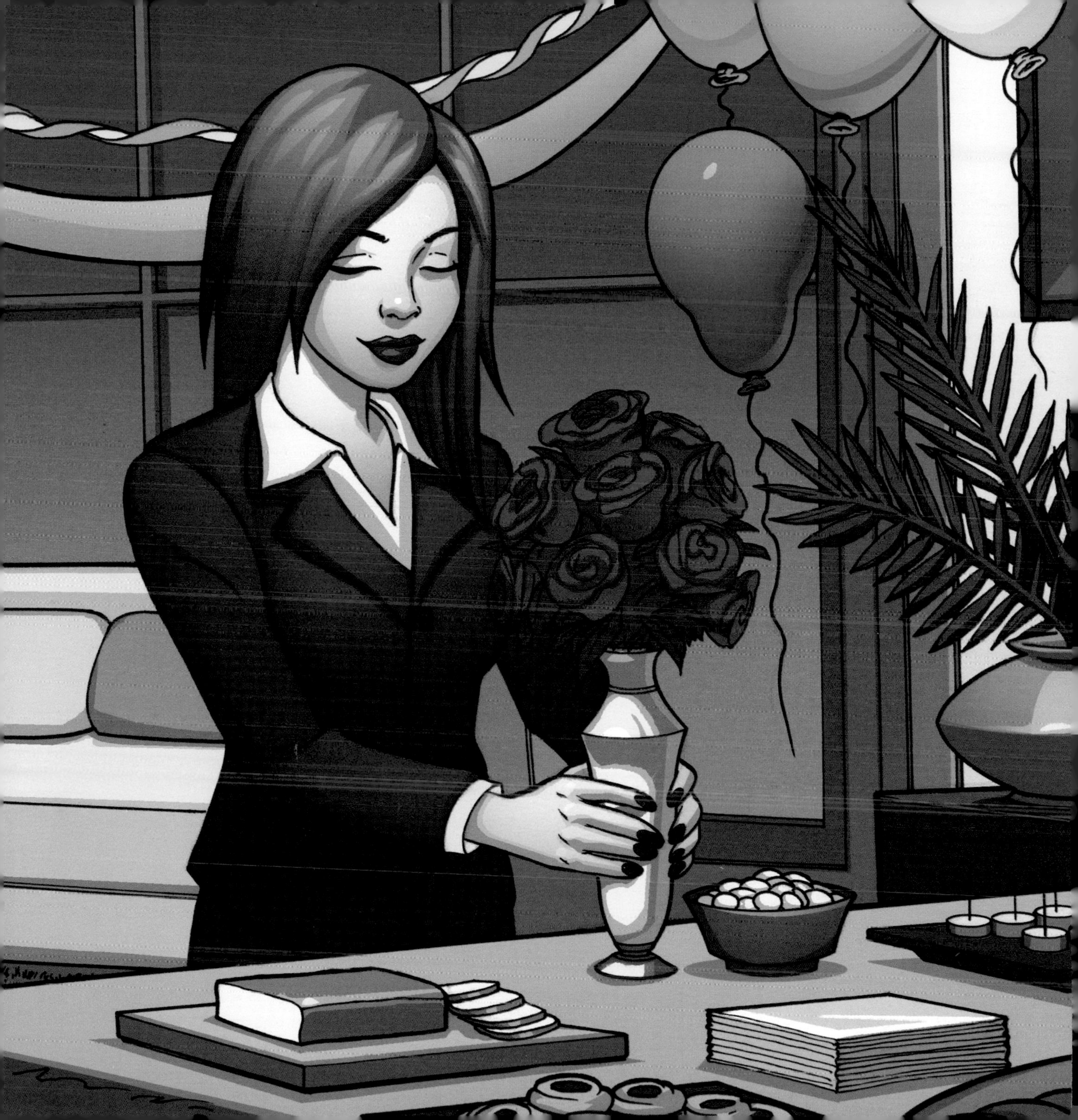

Ding Dong! The doorbell rang.

"Welcome," Rachel said, greeting Bruce's friends. Many of them were wealthy, like Bruce, and the ladies were dripping with diamonds and pearls.

Soon everyone was there—including Bruce's business partner, Lucius Fox, and Bruce's butler, Alfred.

The only person missing was Bruce.

Rachel peeked out the window. A limousine was in front of the building.

"He's coming!" Rachel shouted.

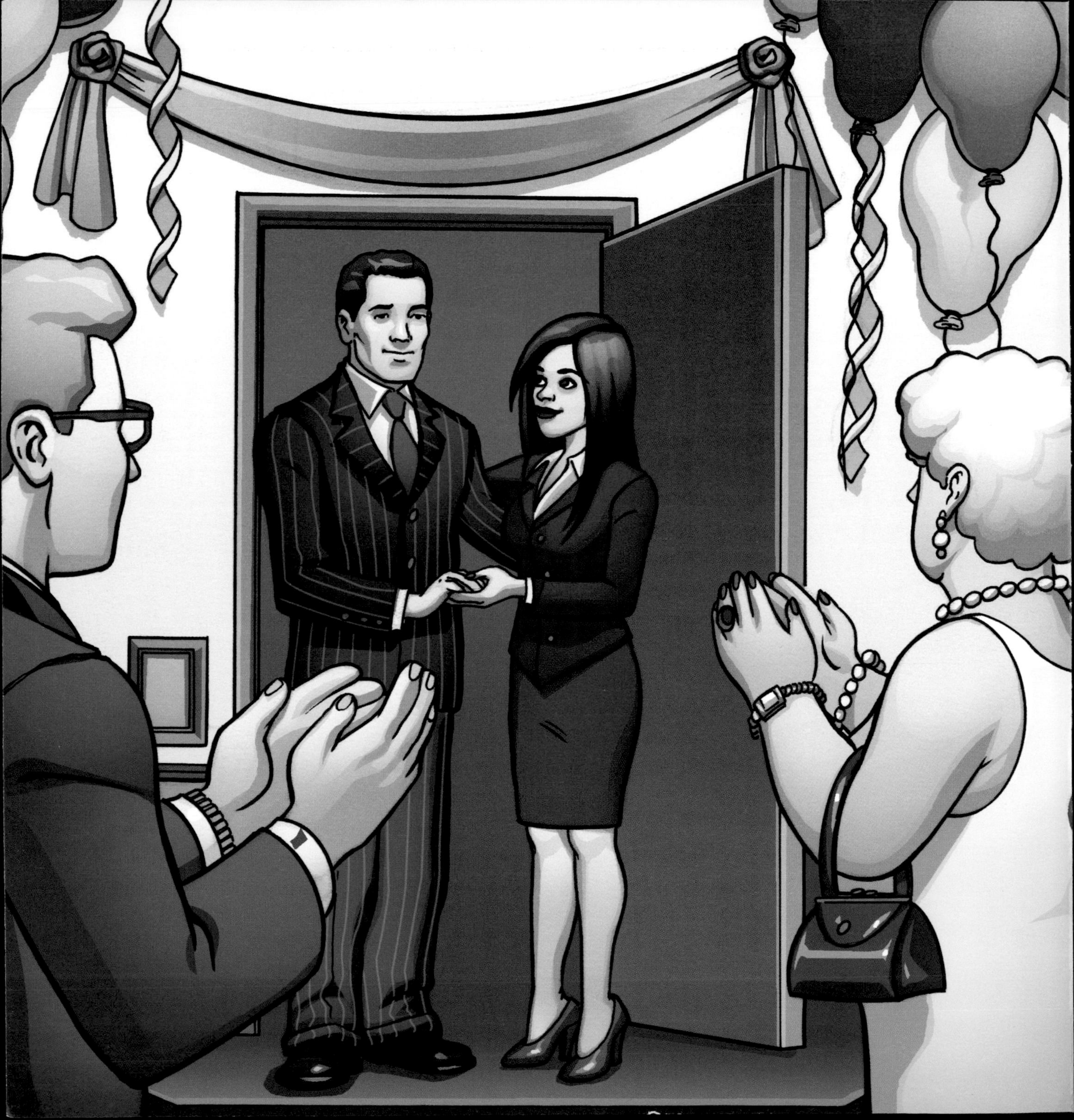

"Surprise!" everyone yelled as Bruce came through the door.
"Happy birthday!" Rachel said.
Bruce looked around the room and turned to Rachel. "This is the best birthday ever!" he said. "Thank you!"

Rachel brought out a cake with candles glowing on top.
"To Bruce," she said. "A great friend to everyone in Gotham!" The
guests cheered, and Bruce blushed. "You shouldn't have," he said.

But not *everyone* in Gotham wanted Bruce to have a happy birthday.

The Joker and his goons suddenly burst through Rachel's door. "Surprise!" the Joker cackled. "Did somebody order clowns for this party?"

The Joker was Gotham's most dangerous villain. He couldn't resist crashing a party full of the city's wealthiest citizens.

As soon as Bruce saw the Joker, he slipped out of the room.

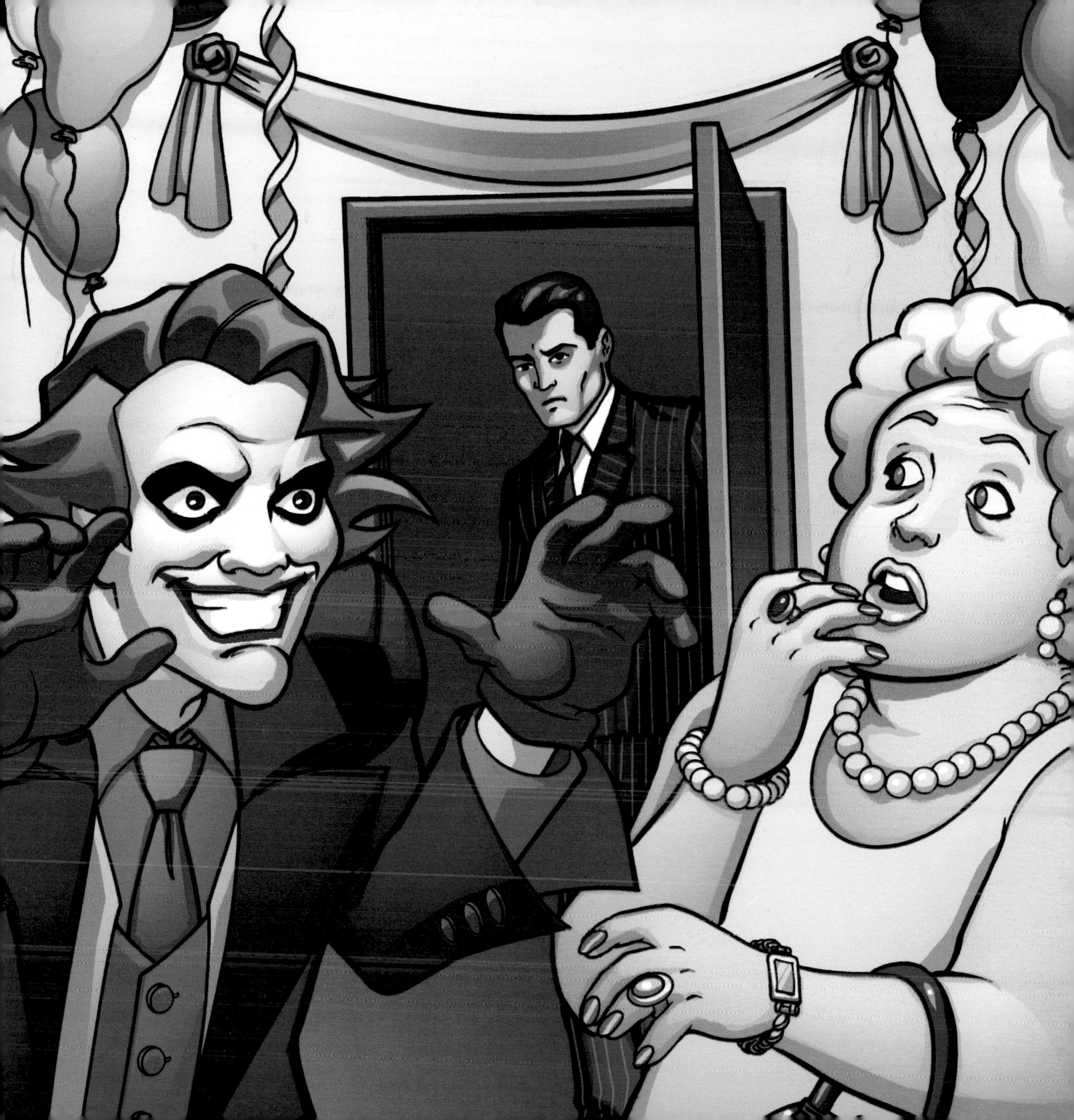

The guests tried to run, but the Joker set off a
smoke bomb that filled the room with sleeping gas.

One by one the guests fell to the floor in a deep sleep. "Get to work!" the Joker shouted. His men began snatching jewelry, watches, and wallets from the slumbering party guests.

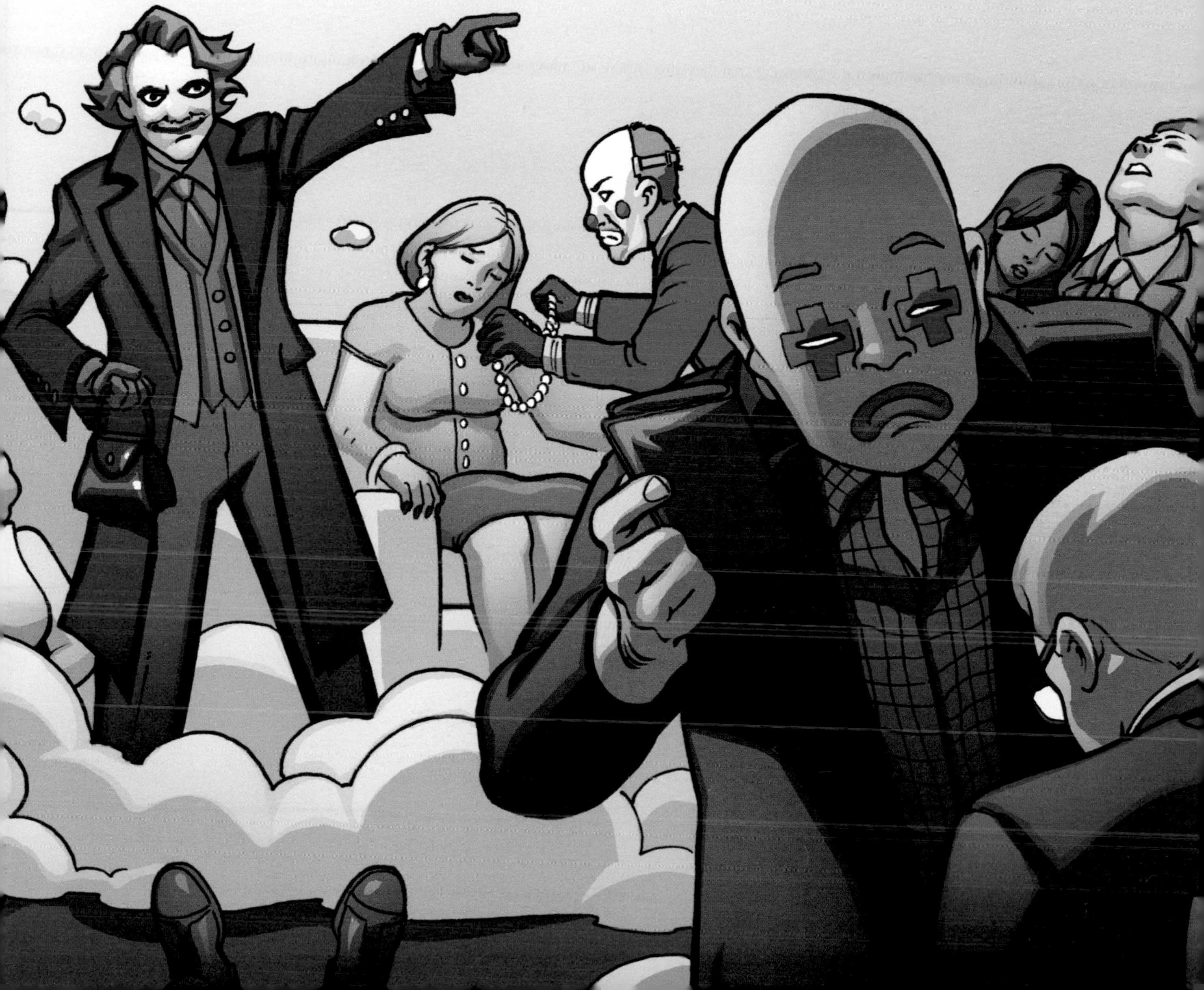

Rachel coughed as the gas filled her lungs. "Stop," she choked. But the Joker just laughed.

Finally, the gas was too much. Rachel fell asleep.

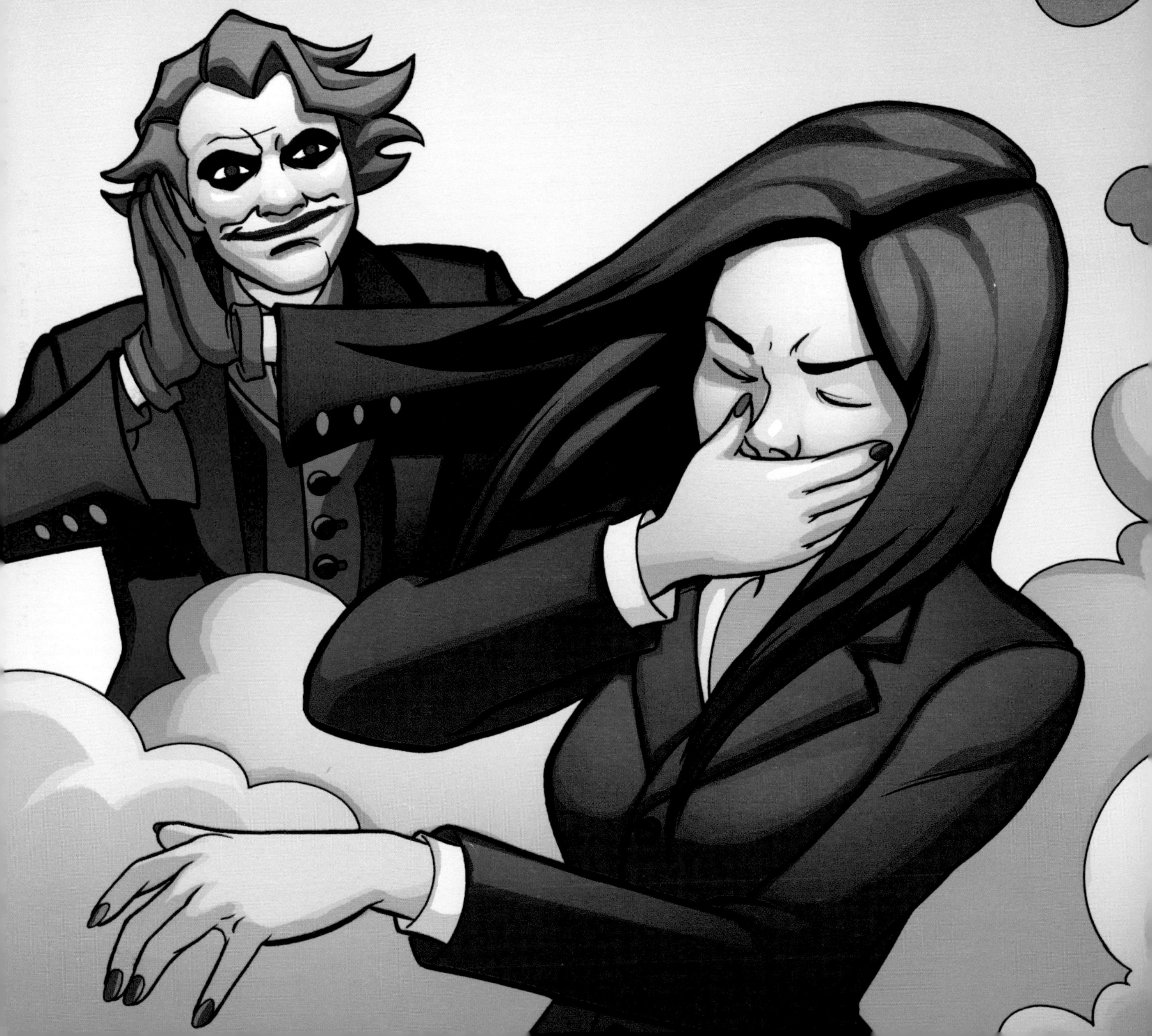

One of the Joker's goons heaved her over his shoulder. He knew Bruce Wayne would pay a big ransom for his friend. He started to walk out the door.

"Let her go!" a voice boomed. The Joker and his men turned to see—BATMAN!

"Well, isn't *this* a surprise," the Joker said.

Batman wanted to catch the Joker, but first he had to save Rachel.

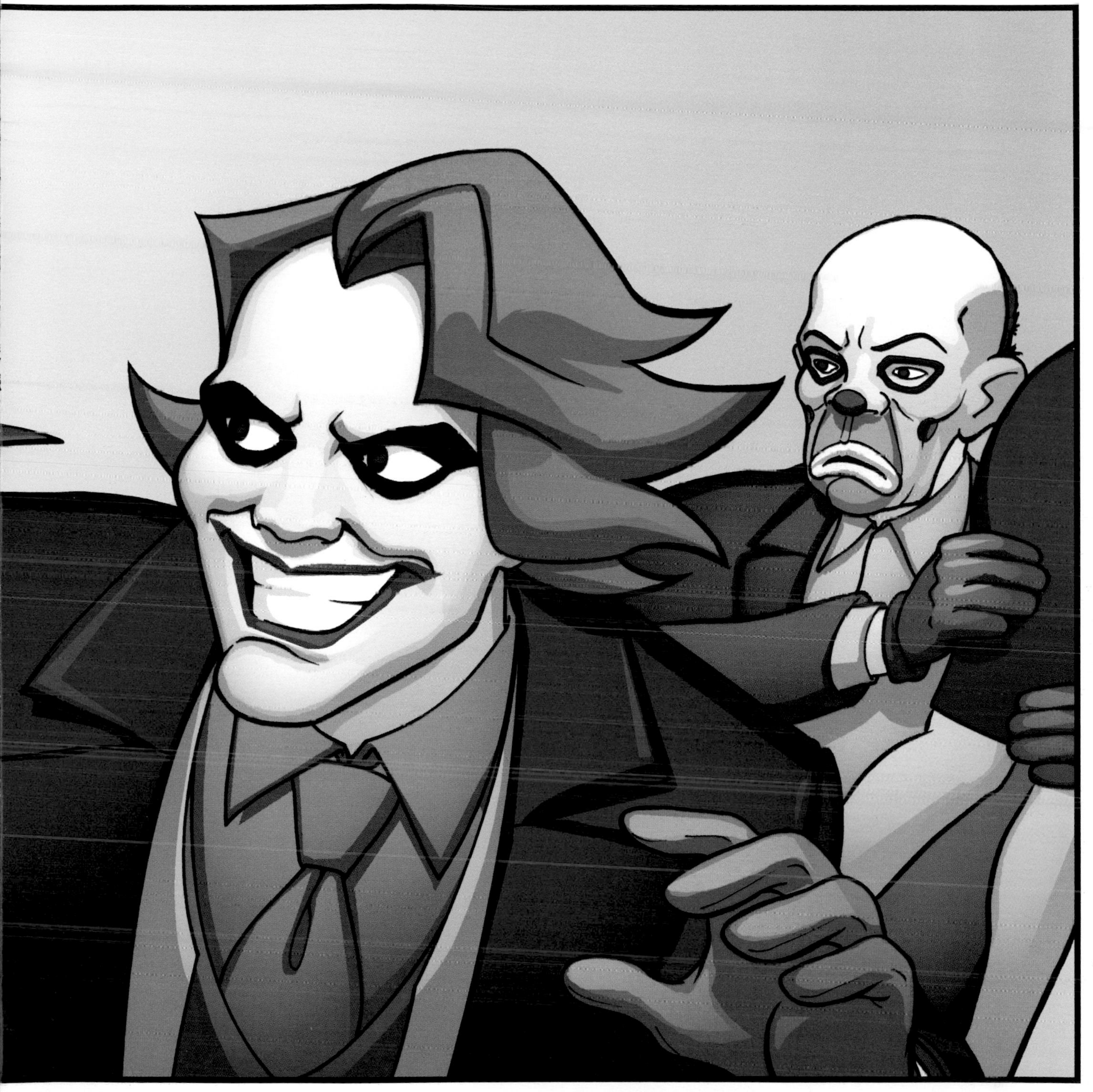

The goon with Rachel turned to run, but he didn't get far.
Batman quickly grabbed another clown and threw him across
the room at his partner in crime.

As the thugs fell, Batman leaped forward and caught the sleeping Rachel. Now it was time to catch the Joker!

Batman turned to face his enemy—but the Joker was gone!
He had escaped while Batman was rescuing Rachel.

Rachel and the other party guests slowly began to wake up. They saw their hero, Batman. He had saved the day again!

The people of Gotham were safe for now, but everyone
knew the Joker would be back with more nasty surprises.
They also knew Batman would be ready.